A Joyful Christmas

A Treasury of New and Classic Songs, Poems, and Stories for the Holiday

Collected and Illustrated by
JAMES RANSOME

Christy Ottaviano Books
Henry Holt and Company • New York

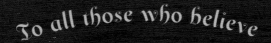

To all those who believe

Permission to reproduce the following is gratefully acknowledged:

"Christmas Eve at Indian Lake" © 2010 by Joseph Bruchac; "A Time of Angels" © 2010 by Joyce Hansen;
"Maybe in Bethlehem," "How I Know," and "Christmas Gift" © 2010 by Margaret Hillert;
"The History of Christmas" © 2010 by Deborah Hopkinson; "Ms. MacAdoo's Christmas Guests" © 2010 by Gloria Houston;
"On a Christmas Night," from *The Collected Poems of Langston Hughes* by Langston Hughes, edited by Arnold Rampersad with
David Roessel, Associate Editor, © 1994 by the Estate of Langston Hughes, used by permission of Alfred A. Knopf, a division
of Random House, Inc.; "The Blind Ox" © 2010 by Tony Johnston; "Miracle at Midnight" © 2010 by Katherine Paterson;
"There Was No Snow on Christmas Eve" © 2010 by Pam Muñoz Ryan; "Dear Santa" © 2010 by Heidi E. Y. Stemple;
"Christmas-in-a-Shoe-box" © 2010 by Ella Joyce Stewart; "A Carol for the Shepherds" © 2010 by Nancy Willard;
"A Christmas Gift" © 2010 by Cedric Williams.

Henry Holt and Company, LLC, *Publishers since 1866*
175 Fifth Avenue, New York, New York 10010 [www.HenryHoltKids.com]

Henry Holt® is a registered trademark of Henry Holt and Company, LLC.
Compilation and illustrations copyright © 2010 by James E. Ransome
All rights reserved.
Distributed in Canada by H. B. Fenn and Company Ltd.

Library of Congress Cataloging-in-Publication Data
A Joyful Christmas : a treasury of new and classic songs, poems, and stories for the holiday /
compiled and illustrated by James E. Ransome. — 1st ed.
p. cm.
ISBN 978-0-8050-6621-0
1. Christmas—Literary collections. 2. American literature—21st century. I. Ransome, James.
PS509.C56A435   2010   810'.8'033—dc22   2009029319

First Edition—2010 / Designed by Elynn Cohen
The artist used oils on paper to create the illustrations for this book.
Printed in June 2010 in China by South China Printing Company Ltd.,
Dongguan City, Guangdong Province, on acid-free paper. ∞

1 3 5 7 9 10 8 6 4 2

A Note from James Ransome

I've always cherished Christmas treasuries and can remember many holiday seasons in the family room with the kids enjoying a Christmas anthology, singing favorite songs, and looking at beautiful illustrations. Through the years my collection has grown, and when I literally couldn't fit another on our bookshelf, I approached my editor, Christy Ottaviano, with the idea of creating my own compilation. Once she agreed, the real work began. I knew it would take time to gather the pieces; I just never imagined it would take a decade.

Early on, I decided to divide my compilation into two sections: Soul and Heart. Soul is understood as the moral, emotional nature of a human being; the spiritual essence of life. This section consists of songs, stories, and poems that celebrate the birth of Jesus and the historical significance of the Christmas holiday. Giving gifts began at the stable with the generous offerings from the three kings to the baby Jesus. This symbol of giving has become the cornerstone of today's Christmas celebration.

Heart is the central, vital, main part of life; the essence or core. This second half summarizes what makes Christmas special today. Bridging the two sections is a piece by Deborah Hopkinson, entitled "The History of Christmas," which provides an understanding about how tinsels, cookies, sparkling lights, and pine trees became part of our Christmas holiday.

My collection isn't just a gathering of well-known Christmas songs, poems, and stories. *A Joyful Christmas* is a combination of popular Christmas favorites and newly published poems and stories from some of the country's most established children's book writers. My only direction to the contributors was that they write whatever they wished as long as it celebrated the birth of Christ and the Christmas holiday. Many of these authors are my friends and I cannot thank them enough for their wonderful pieces, which have made *A Joyful Christmas* a truly special collection.

Merry Christmas to you and yours.

James Ransome

Contents

Soul

The moral or emotional nature of a human being, a spiritual
or emotional warmth; an essential part, quality, or principle

A Time of Angels

Joyce Hansen

Long ago in the city of Galilee, a young woman prepared for her wedding day. Her mind was filled with wonderful dreams of the new life she would share with her husband-to-be, Joseph. However, God had other plans for Mary—wondrous things that she could not have dreamt of.

In the middle of her wedding preparations, a man she'd never seen before came to her door. "Greetings," the man said. "God loves you above all others. The Lord is with you."

Mary was shocked and a little frightened. What a strange way of saying hello, she thought.

As if he could read her mind, the man declared, "Fear not, Mary. God loves you. You will shortly have a baby. You will name him Jesus. He shall be great and shall be called the Son of the Most High."

Mary trembled slightly. How did this stranger know her name? She stared at him with a confused look in her eyes. "How can I have a baby? I have not yet married Joseph."

"With God all things are possible. The Holy Spirit shall touch you. The child you give birth to shall be called holy—the Son of God."

Mary's mind opened slowly, like the petals of a bud, as she began to understand. She looked at her visitor with a calm and steady gaze. Mary realized that the man was an angel sent by God. "I am the Lord's servant," she said. "I believe everything you say. I will do God's will."

The angel, whose name was Gabriel, disappeared as mysteriously as he had appeared, and Mary's life was changed forever. When she told Joseph about the visit from the angel and the holy baby she would give birth to, he didn't believe her. Joseph was angry and no longer wanted to marry her. Yet, because he was a kind and fair man, he decided to not tell anyone that Mary was having another man's child. He didn't want to shame her, so he would quietly leave her.

But an angel of the Lord spoke to Joseph in a dream saying, "Joseph, do not fear to take Mary for your wife. Her baby is from the Holy Spirit; she will give birth to a son, and you shall call him Jesus for he will save his people from their sins."

When Joseph awoke from his sleep, he did as the angel ordered him to and married Mary. The couple's troubles were not over, though. At that time, the Roman ruler of Galilee and other cities ordered people to return to the towns and neighborhoods where they'd been born so that they could be taxed. Therefore, Joseph had to travel to his birthplace, the city of Bethlehem. Mary had to go along with him.

The journey to Bethlehem was long and grueling, especially for Mary, who would soon give birth. Doubt and fear must have traveled with the couple. Only their faith in God's word kept Mary and Joseph strong during their arduous journey through the desert.

The night they reached Bethlehem, Mary knew that her time had come. Joseph was relieved when they entered the city and found an inn—a perfect resting place for the young mother to give birth and for the weary couple to rest. But there was no room at the inn.

Joseph, in desperation, found a stable near the inn. And so, amid oxen and sheep, Mary gave birth to a son, just as the angel said she would. She lovingly wrapped her baby in swaddling cloths and laid him in a manger—a feeding trough for the animals—filled with straw.

At this time also, shepherds watching their flocks in the field saw a great and blinding light in the night sky. At first they were terrified. But the light began to swerve and sway and change form, until they recognized the shape of an angel.

"Be not afraid; for behold, I bring you good news," the angel announced. "To you is born this day in the city of David a savior, who is Christ the Lord. You will find the baby lying in a manger."

The shepherds' mouths opened in wonder as suddenly the entire midnight sky became as bright as day with the light of a thousand angels. They listened in awe as the angels sang "Glory to God in the highest, and on earth peace among men."

When the angels left, the shepherds hurried to Bethlehem to find this holy baby lying in a manger. They were not the only people traveling to the stable in Bethlehem. Wise men in the East had seen a magnificent star and understood its meaning— the holy baby had been born. They too journeyed to Bethlehem and carried gifts of gold, frankincense, and myrrh for the baby.

Simple shepherds and wise men alike worshipped a little baby lying in a lowly manger. They saw the glory of God and praised His son on earth. This was the first Christmas.

Silent Night

Joseph Mohr and Franz Grüber
translated by Reverend John Young

Si - lent night, ho - ly night, All is calm, all is bright.

'Round yon vir - gin moth-er and child, Ho-ly In-fant, so ten-der and mild,

Sleep in heav-en-ly peace, Sleep in heav-en-ly peace.

2. Silent night, holy night,
   Shepherds quake at the sight;
   Glories stream from heaven afar,
   Heav'nly hosts sing "Alleluia!"
   Christ, the Savior, is born,
   Christ, the Savior is born.

3. Silent night, holy night,
   Son of God, love's pure light;
   Radiant beams from Thy holy face,
   With the dawn of redeeming grace,
   Jesus, Lord, at Thy birth,
   Jesus, Lord, at Thy birth.

The Friendly Beasts

English, traditional

Jesus, our brother, strong and good,
Was humbly born in a stable rude,
And the friendly beasts around Him stood,
Jesus, our brother, strong and good.

"I," said the donkey, shaggy and brown,
"I carried His mother up hill and down,
I carried her safely to Bethlehem town;
I," said the donkey, shaggy and brown.

"I," said the cow, all white and red,
"I gave Him my manger for His bed,
I gave Him my hay to pillow His head;
I," said the cow, all white and red.

"I," said the sheep with the curly horn,
"I gave Him my wool for His blanket warm,
He wore my coat on Christmas morn;
I," said the sheep with the curly horn.

"I," said the dove, from the rafters high,
"Cooed Him to sleep, my mate and I;
We cooed Him to sleep, my mate and I;
I," said the dove, from the rafters high.

And every beast by some good spell,
In the stable dark was glad to tell,
Of the gift he gave Immanuel,
The gift he gave to Immanuel.

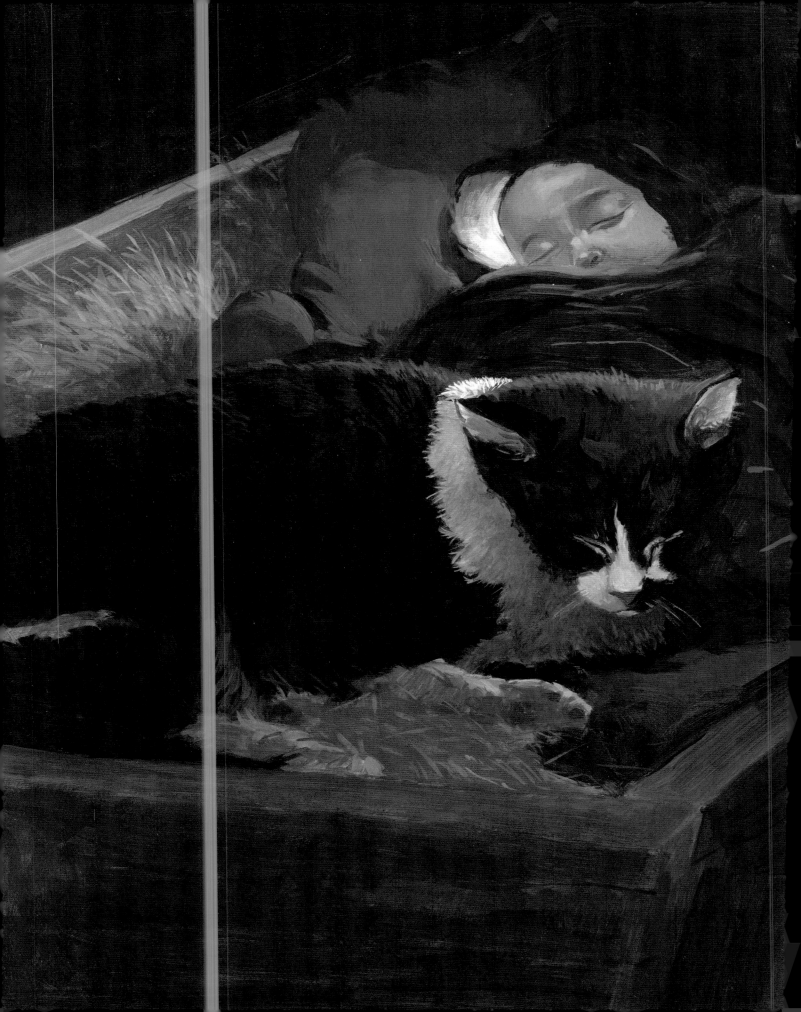

Maybe in Bethlehem

Margaret Hillert

The ass was there in Bethlehem,
And flocks of woolly sheep,
But I like to think a little cat
Purred the Babe to sleep.

An ox was there and other beasts
Too large to come too near.
But a little cat could curl up close
And cause the Child no fear.

And maybe Jesus clutched its fur,
And maybe Mary smiled
To see the small one lying there
Beside the Holy Child.

A Carol for the Shepherds

Nancy Willard

An angel woke three shepherds
with timbrel, harp, and drum.
"The morning stars are singing,
the planets dance and hum.
So take yourselves to Bethlehem.
The Prince of Peace has come."

The sheep scattered behind them.
The crags were dark and wide.
"The wolves will surely find them.
We will not leave their side
for all the babes in Bethlehem,"
the frightened shepherds cried.

The angel sang, "O Morning Bright,"
and from his sleeve let fall
a hundred stars, and by their light
the frightened shepherds saw
the wolf that watched their flocks by night
was caring for them all.

"Tonight the rivers sing for joy,
the very stones have tongues,
the lion and the lamb lie down,
the moon marries the sun.
So take yourselves to Bethlehem.
The Prince of Peace has come."

The Blind Ox

Tony Johnston

The blind ox is restless tonight.
In his stall he shuffles his heavy feet.
He snuffles the straw.
He cannot eat.

The boy is restless tonight.
He soothes the ox,
"So, so."
He cannot sleep.

Outside, a strange thing calls.
Slow, slow, they go
into the night.

And the night is lit with
silence.
And the night is lit with
stars.

The blind ox sways
like a great stone cart.
The boy stays at his side,
one hand always
on his flank.

The ox stumbles
as he goes.
The boy too.
Over a clump of grass
or perhaps into a hole
where some small creature sleeps.
"So, so."
Stumbling boy, stumbling ox.

And the night is lit with
silence.
And the night is lit with
hope.

In his old head the ox knows
something.
Perhaps he smells the light
of the stars.
He plods so sure a path
the boy keeps walking,
trusting.

The land glows silver.
As the ox plows along,
cloud-eyed and slow,
his hooves raise a shining
dust.

The ox steps on a loose stone
and sinks to his knees.
The boy too,
one hand ever on the flank.
"So, so."

Briefly they rest
beneath the starry fields
of sky.
Kneeling ox, kneeling boy.

*And the night is lit with
wonder.
And the night is lit with
stars.*

The ox cannot see, but he knows
the way.
Slow, slow they go this night.
In their hearts they want
to run.
Slow, slow they walk
into the barn
sweet with smells of milk
and dung.

The ox trembles.
The boy trembles too.

In their own dark they feel great joy.
They grope their way
close to the Child—
blind ox, blind boy.

We Three Kings of Orient Are

John Henry Hopkins Jr.

2. Born a babe on Bethlehem's plain,
   Gold we bring to crown Him again;
   King forever, ceasing never,
   Over us all to reign.

Chorus

O star of wonder, star of night,
star with royal beauty bright,
westward leading, still proceeding,
guide us to thy perfect light.

What You Gonna Name That Pretty Little Baby?

Negro spiritual

Oh, Mary, what you gonna name
That pretty little baby?
Glory, glory, glory
To the newborn King!
Some will call Him one thing,
But I think I'll call Him Jesus.
Glory, glory, glory
To the newborn King!
Some will call Him one thing,
But I think I'll say Immanuel.
Glory, glory, glory
To the newborn King!

What Can I Give Him?

Christina Rossetti

What can I give Him,
Poor as I am?
If I were a shepherd,
I would bring a lamb;
If I were a wise man,
I would do my part—
Yet what I can I give Him,
Give my heart.

Long, Long Ago

Unknown

Winds through the olive trees
Softly did blow,
Round little Bethlehem
Long, long ago.

Sheep on hillside lay
Whiter than snow;
Shepherds were watching them,
Long, long ago.

Then from the happy sky,
Angels bent low,
Singing their songs of joy,
Long, long ago.

For in a manger bed,
Cradled we know,
Christ came to Bethlehem,
Long, long ago.

There Was No Snow on Christmas Eve

Pam Muñoz Ryan

There was no snow on Christmas Eve
Or snowflakes in a flurry dance.
No pristine banks of milky white
Or ice pond in a shivery scene.
There was no bitter winter wind,
No need for woolen caps and gloves.
So long ago in Bethlehem,
Instead of storm, a night serene.

There was no snow on Christmas Eve
When burro took them through the street.
Sweet Mary wore a lightweight robe
And Joseph, sandals on his feet.
A stable opened to the world.
Their quilt? No more than supple straw.
The balmy season, bright with Star,
Let shepherds dream among the sheep.

There was no snow on Christmas Eve
Instead a desert zephyr blew
And palm fronds sang a rustling tune
To welcome the awaited birth.
From mouse to camel gathered near,
Wise men and women warm of heart,
And barefoot children—all to see
Why angels sang above the earth.

On a Christmas Night

Langston Hughes

In Bethlehem on a Christmas night
All around the Child shone a holy light.
All around His head was a halo bright
On a Christmas night.

"We have no room," the innkeeper called,
So the glory fell where the cows were stalled,
But among the guests were Three Kings who called
On a Christmas night.

How can it be such a light shines here
In this humble stable once cold and drear?
Oh, the Child has come to bring good cheer
On a Christmas night!

And what is the name of the little One?
His name is Jesus—He's God's own Son.
Be happy, happy, everyone
On a Christmas night!

Joy to the World

George Frideric Handel and Lowell Mason;
lyrics by Isaac Watts

2. Joy to the world! the Savior reigns;
   Let men their songs employ;
   While fields and floods, rocks,
      hills and plains
   Repeat the sounding joy,
   Repeat the sounding joy,
   Repeat, repeat the sounding joy.

3. He rules the world with truth
      and grace,
   And makes the nations prove
   The glories of His righteousness,
   And wonders of His love,
   And wonders of His love,
   And wonders, and wonders of
      His love.

The History of Christmas

Deborah Hopkinson

"O Christmas tree,
O Christmas tree!"

Toys and bright tinsel, cookies and carols, sparkling lights and pine-scented trees. All these things make Christmas special. How did the celebration of the birth of one child so long ago come to include so many different traditions?

People have celebrated the birth of Jesus on December 25 since the fourth century. But the Bible doesn't tell us the exact date of his birth. Most historians don't think Jesus was born in December at all, as it would have been too cold then for the shepherds to be keeping watch over their sheep at night.

But it was natural for the early Christians to choose December 25 as the birthday of the Christ child. The Roman emperor Constantine became a Christian in the year 312. He decided to combine the celebration of the birth of the sun god, which the Romans celebrated on December 25, with the worship of Christ, who also brought light into the world.

There were other reasons, too. The winter solstice, marking the shortest day of the year, took place just a few days before December 25 and was already a time of celebration in Europe. Families came together at the end of the harvest season to feast, dance, and sing. The rich sometimes gave gifts to the poor peasants. These celebrations at the darkest time of the year brought light and hope that spring would come again soon.

It's likely that the tradition of the Christmas tree and decorating with evergreens has its roots in this period, too. People have long prized evergreens because they stay green and fresh even in winter. The earliest record of a decorated Christmas tree in a house dates back to 1605 in Germany. German settlers and soldiers brought the custom to America during the Revolutionary War. Gradually, Christmas trees began to appear all over America.

Many of our other Christmas traditions come from England. In the 1840s, English people became worried that the ancient customs were being forgotten. They wanted to bring charity, hope, and love back into Christmas. Singing Christmas carols became popular, and Queen Victoria herself made Christmas special for her children.

Children have been at the center of Christmas ever since. For many of them, the best part of Christmas is Santa Claus, who is also called Saint Nicholas and Father Christmas. And Christmas just wouldn't be the same without this jolly old man who, each Christmas Eve, gets into his sleigh and flies straight into our hearts.

Heart

The central, vital, or main part;
real meaning; essence; core

December

Aileen Fisher

I like days
with a snow-white collar,
and nights when the moon
is a silver dollar,
and hills are filled
with eiderdown stuffing
and your breath makes smoke
like an engine puffing.

I like days
when feathers are snowing
and all the eaves
have petticoats showing,
and the air is cold
and the wires are humming,
but you feel all warm . . .
with Christmas coming.

How I Know

Margaret Hillert

How do I know it's Christmastime?
How can I always tell?
Bells there are that suddenly chime,
Wonderful things to smell,
People and packages, secrets and song,
Holly wreaths at the door,
Colored lights as we drive along,
Santas in every store,
Carols and cookies and candy canes,
Mysterious things to hide,
Snowflakes glowing through windowpanes,
And a lovely feeling inside.

We Wish You a Merry Christmas

Traditional English Carol

2. Now bring us some figgy pudding,
   Now bring us some figgy pudding,
   Now bring us some figgy pudding,
   And bring it out here.
   Refrain

3. We won't go until we get some,
   We won't go until we get some,
   We won't go until we get some,
   So bring some out here.
   Refrain

4. We all love figgy pudding,
   We all love figgy pudding,
   We all love figgy pudding,
   So bring some out here.
   Refrain

5. We wish you a merry Christmas,
   We wish you a merry Christmas,
   We wish you a merry Christmas,
   And a happy New Year!
   Refrain

A Visit from Saint Nicholas

Clement C. Moore

'Twas the night before Christmas, when all through the house
Not a creature was stirring, not even a mouse;
The stockings were hung by the chimney with care,
In hopes that Saint Nicholas soon would be there;
The children were nestled all snug in their beds,
While visions of sugarplums danced in their heads;
And Mamma in her kerchief, and I in my cap,
Had just settled our brains for a long winter's nap;

When out on the lawn there arose such a clatter,
I sprang from the bed to see what was the matter.
Away to the window I flew like a flash,
Tore open the shutters and threw up the sash.
The moon on the breast of the newfallen snow,
Gave the luster of midday to objects below,
When, what to my wondering eyes should appear,
But a miniature sleigh, and eight tiny reindeer,

With a little old driver, so lively and quick,
I knew in a moment it must be Saint Nick.
More rapid than eagles his coursers they came,
And he whistled, and shouted, and called them by name;
"Now, *Dasher!* now, *Dancer!* now, *Prancer!* and *Vixen!*
On, *Comet!* on, *Cupid!* on, *Donder* and *Blitzen!*
To the top of the porch! to the top of the wall!
Now dash away! dash away! dash away all!"

As dry leaves that before the wild hurricane fly,
When they meet with an obstacle, mount to the sky;
So up to the housetop the coursers they flew,
With the sleigh full of toys, and Saint Nicholas too.
And then, in a twinkling, I heard on the roof,
The prancing and pawing of each little hoof—
As I drew in my head, and was turning around,
Down the chimney Saint Nicholas came with a bound.

He was dressed all in fur from his head to his foot,
And his clothes were all tarnished with ashes and soot;
A bundle of toys he had flung on his back,
And he looked like a peddler just opening his pack.
His eyes—how they twinkled! his dimples how merry!
His cheeks were like roses, his nose like a cherry!
His droll little mouth was drawn up like a bow,
And the beard of his chin was as white as the snow;

The stump of a pipe he held tight in his teeth,
And the smoke it encircled his head like a wreath;
He had a broad face and a little round belly,
That shook, when he laughed, like a bowlful of jelly.
He was chubby and plump, a right jolly old elf,
And I laughed when I saw him, in spite of myself;
A wink of his eye and a twist of his head,
Soon gave me to know I had nothing to dread;

He spoke not a word, but went straight to his work,
And filled all the stockings; then turned with a jerk,
And laying his finger aside of his nose
And giving a nod, up the chimney he rose;
He sprang to his sleigh, to his team gave a whistle,
And away they all flew like the down of a thistle,
But I heard him exclaim, ere he drove out of sight,
"Happy Christmas to all, and to all a good night!"

Dear Santa

Heidi E. Y. Stemple

Dear Santa,
I've been very good this year,
   so, here's what I want for Christmas:
I want a baby sister or brother.
But not a noisy one like Mollie got last year.
I want one that I can play with and dress up.
If you don't bring me a baby for Christmas,
   I'll take a puppy.
I also want a Barbie jeep
   and a dollhouse.
                    Sincerely,
                    Maddy Jane Pratt

Dear Santa,
Mommy says you're not in charge of
   baby brothers and sisters.
I know she's making that up,
   so I just wanted to remind you.
I've decided that I want the baby
   to be a girl named Alison.
Also, I want a canopy bed like Mollie has.
                    Sincerely,
                    Maddy Jane Pratt

Dear Santa,
What I meant when I said
   I wanted a sister
   was a baby.
I guess I wasn't very clear because
   Mommy said the girl we met yesterday
   named Kate
   is going to be my new sister.
Well, not a *real* sister.
A *foster* sister.
And she is fourteen!
Can I at least get a puppy
   since you messed up so bad?
                    Sincerely,
                    Maddy Jane Pratt

Dear Santa,
We picked up Kate at the county girls' home today.
She's okay,
    but I can't dress her up
    or carry her around.
She is very polite and kind of shy.
I heard her crying in her room.
And she doesn't celebrate Christmas.
She says she doesn't believe in holidays.
Now that she's my foster sister,
    does that mean that I can't celebrate Christmas either?
Then, you can take her back.
I'd rather have Christmas.
            Sincerely,
            Maddy Jane Pratt

Dear Santa,
Kate doesn't really have much stuff.
When you bring all my presents
    could you bring her a couple things too?
Even if she doesn't believe in Christmas,
I bet she still believes in presents.
            Sincerely,
            Maddy Jane Pratt

Dear Santa,
I heard Kate crying again at night.
I think she is sad.
She doesn't have any stuffed animals.
Could you bring her one for Christmas?
That would be good.
I don't cry at night
    when I have Timmy the Bear
    with me.

            Sincerely,
            Maddy Jane Pratt

Dear Santa,
Mollie helped me wrap
    Timmy the Bear in red and silver paper.
We put a giant green bow on the top.
I'm going to put him under the tree for Kate.
If it wouldn't be too much trouble,
    could you bring me
    a new favorite bear?
                Thanks,
                Maddy Jane Pratt

Dear Santa,
    At first, Kate just sat on the sofa
        and watched us open our presents.
    Hers just waited, still wrapped,
        under the tree in a big colorful pile.
    But, when I brought out
        Timmy the Bear
    all wrapped up in the red and silver paper,
    she opened him up so carefully,
        she didn't make one rip.
    And then she cried.
    But, it wasn't the same sad cry as before.
    I think she really likes being my sister now.
    Foster, but real.
    And even if I can't dress her up
        or carry her around,
    she is the best Christmas gift I ever got.
Thank you, Santa.
I'll write again next year.
                With love,
                Maddy Jane Pratt

Jingle, Bells

James Pierpont

Christmas Eve at Indian Lake

Joseph Bruchac

Sabael stands with open hands
beside the frozen lake.
He knows that giving always gives us
more than what we take.

A small spruce tree is hung with seeds
and fruit, his gift each year.
Bright corn is spread upon the ground,
good food for Brother Deer.

He gives thanks for that perfect child
who loves both Indian and white,
who knows the gentle and the wild
stand equal in Creation's sight.

"*Ktsi Oleohneh*," he sings,
"Great Sazos Klist, for all these things,
for snow and deer, for trees and breath,
for life that goes on after death."

He lifts his gaze up toward the sky.
The Milky Way catches his eye.
He wonders, Should my feet begin
to walk that Sky Trail into Heaven?

Then the night wind starts to bring
the sound of grandchildren as they sing
"Silent Night" from his cabin on the hill.
Sabael smiles. He'll join them, still.

Ktsi Oleohneh (Kit-see Oh-lee-oh-nee): Abenaki for "great thanks."
Sazos Klist (Sah-zohs Kleest): Abenaki for Jesus Christ.

Once There Was a Snowman

Anonymous

Once there was a snowman
    Who stood outside the door.
He wished that he could come inside
    And run about the floor.
He wished that he could warm himself
    Beside the fire, so red.
He wished that he could climb
    Upon the big white bed.

So he called to the North Wind,
    "Come and help me, pray,
For I'm completely frozen
    Standing out here all day."
So the North Wind came along
    And blew him in the door,
And now there's nothing left of him
    But a puddle on the floor!

Day Before Christmas

Marchette Chute

We have been helping with the cake
And licking out the pan,
And wrapping up our packages
As neatly as we can.
We have hung our stockings up
Beside the open grate,
And now there's nothing more to do
Except
To
Wait.

Christmas Gift

Margaret Hillert

I looked and looked until I found
The nicest gift of all.
I tiptoed in without a sound
And hurried down the hall.
I wrapped it up and tied it well
And hid it on the shelf.
I'm so afraid that I might tell,
I'd better hide myself.

A Christmas Gift

Cedric Williams

"Pssst!" Kenny whispered as he slowly tiptoed into his mother's bedroom.

"Kenny, do you know what time it is?" his mother mumbled while trying to hide under her covers and avoid opening her eyes.

"It's Christmas mornin' time, Momma," Kenny said with a smile as he eagerly climbed into her big, soft bed.

"It's five thirty in the morning," his mother mumbled from beneath her fluffy pile of pillows and blankets. "And that's much too early for little boys to be out of bed and tiptoeing about, even on Christmas."

"But I want to see if I got the gift I wanted from Santa!" Kenny replied as he jumped off the bed and began to sing and dance around the room.

"Jingle, bells! Jingle, bells! Jingle all the way . . ."

Upon hearing that, Kenny's mother slowly poked her head out from beneath her covers and gazed sadly at her son. Unlike Kenny, she was already sure that Santa had not been to their home the night before. Not because Kenny was a bad boy. To the contrary. As a matter of fact, Kenny's mother believed that he was the best little boy in the whole wide world. He was kind to other kids and helped around the house. He did his homework and faithfully took care of his pet mouse. He picked up his clothes off the floor and was always willing to run to the store. Yes, all things considered, Kenny was the best little boy in the whole wide world.

However, difficult events over the previous months—including her separation from Kenny's dad, being unable to find a job, and having to move into a tiny apartment in a strange new city—had left her feeling blue this holiday season. But now, she decided, even if they found nothing from Santa today, they would have a wonderful Christmas celebration anyway.

So, putting her fatigue aside, Kenny's mother jumped out of bed and began to sing and dance with him around the room.

"We wish you a merry Christmas, we wish you a merry Christmas, we wish you a merry Christmas, and a happy New Year!"

For what seemed like hours they danced joyfully from room to room, singing every Christmas song they knew, until finally, exhausted from laughter, they fell to the floor right in front of their tree.

Just as she had guessed, there were no pretty gift boxes waiting to be unwrapped, no

signs of Santa. Feeling sad all over again, Kenny's mother said, "I'm sorry that Santa didn't leave the gift you wanted. Maybe he doesn't know our new address."

With a surprised expression, Kenny looked into his mother's eyes and said, "But, Mommy, I asked Santa for you to feel happy today, so I got just what I wished for." Hearing that, Kenny's mother gave him a cuddle and whispered in his ear, "Just as I've always said, you're the best little boy in the whole wide world."

The Twelve Days of Christmas

Traditional Welsh Carol

On the first day of Christmas
My true love sent to me
A partridge in a pear tree.

Partridge in a pear tree: Partridges will pretend to be injured to lure predators away from their young. The partridge is a symbol of the love and sacrifice of Jesus.

On the second day of Christmas
My true love sent to me
Two turtledoves
And a partridge in a pear tree.

Two turtledoves: Love and romance are represented by turtledoves who choose a mate for life.

On the third day of Christmas

My true love sent to me
Three French hens,
Two turtledoves,
And a partridge in a pear tree.

The three French hens refer to the Holy Trinity—the Father, the Son, and the Holy Spirit—or to the gifts of the Three Wise Men.

On the fourth day of Christmas

My true love sent to me
Four calling birds,
Three French hens,
Two turtledoves,
And a partridge in a pear tree.

The four calling birds symbolize the four Evangelists—Matthew, Mark, Luke, and John—and their gift of the four gospels.

On the fifth day of Christmas

My true love sent to me
Five gold rings,
Four calling birds,
Three French hens,
Two turtledoves,
And a partridge in a pear tree.

The five golden rings represent the five
books of the Old Testament.

On the sixth day of Christmas

My true love sent to me
Six geese a-laying,
Five gold rings,
Four calling birds,
Three French hens,
Two turtledoves,
And a partridge in a pear tree.

The six geese a-laying represent the six days
of Creation, and eggs are a symbol of life.

On the seventh day of Christmas

My true love sent to me
Seven swans a-swimming,
Six geese a-laying,
Five gold rings,
Four calling birds,
Three French hens,
Two turtledoves,
And a partridge in a pear tree.

Seven swans a-swimming stand for the seven gifts of the Holy Spirit: prophecy, service, teaching, encouragement, giving leadership, and mercy.

On the eighth day of Christmas

My true love sent to me
Eight maids a-milking,
Seven swans a-swimming,
Six geese a-laying,
Five gold rings,
Four calling birds,
Three French hens,
Two turtledoves,
And a partridge in a pear tree.

Eight maids a-milking symbolize the eight beatitudes, which spell out blessings for those who are poor and hungry, both financially and spiritually.

On the ninth day of Christmas

My true love sent to me
Nine ladies dancing,
Eight maids a-milking,
Seven swans a-swimming,
Six geese a-laying,
Five golden rings,
Four calling birds,
Three French hens,
Two turtle doves,
And a partridge in a pear tree.

Nine ladies dancing: Peace, joy, love, goodness, patience, kindness, self-control, gentleness, and faithfulness are the nine fruits of the Holy Spirit.

On the tenth day of Christmas

My true love sent to me
Ten lords a-leaping,
Nine ladies dancing,
Eight maids a-milking,
Seven swans a-swimming,
Six geese a-laying,
Five golden rings,
Four calling birds,
Three French hens,
Two turtle doves,
And a partridge in a pear tree.

The ten lords a-leaping symbolize the Ten Commandments.

On the eleventh day of Christmas

My true love sent to me
Eleven pipers piping,
Ten lords a-leaping,
Nine ladies dancing,
Eight maids a-milking,
Seven swans a-swimming,
Six geese a-laying,
Five golden rings,
Four calling birds,
Three French hens,
Two turtle doves,
And a partridge in a pear tree.

*Eleven pipers piping refers to the eleven
faithful apostles who were true to Jesus.*

On the twelfth day of Christmas,

my true love sent to me
Twelve drummers drumming,
Eleven pipers piping,
Ten lords a-leaping,
Nine ladies dancing,
Eight maids a-milking,
Seven swans a-swimming,
Six geese a-laying,
Five golden rings,
Four calling birds,
Three French hens,
Two turtle doves,
And a partridge in a pear tree.

*Twelve drummers drumming: Catholicism is based on
twelve points of doctrine in the Apostles' Creed.*

Ms. MacAdoo's Christmas Guests

Gloria Houston

Ms. MacAdoo had been teaching music in Irving as long as anyone could remember, for so long that almost no one remembered her real name—they just called her Ms. Mac. She had taught almost every person in town. She taught the mayor to toot his trumpet in the band. The fire chief had sung in every program when he was a boy, until one day his voice changed in the middle of his solo. Every teacher at the school, and even the principal, had been in Ms. Mac's music class.

As the town prepared for the holidays each year, Ms. Mac bought a lovely balsam fir from Ed, who sold the best trees. When they marched down the street to her house on Christmas Eve, everyone called out, "Ms. Mac, won't you join us for Christmas dinner tonight?"

But Ms. Mac always smiled and said, "Thank you, I already have plans."

When she had waved good-bye to Ed and closed the door, Ms. Mac took a box, gaily decorated with red and gold and blue, down from its special corner in the closet. Gently she lifted off the top to look inside. Taking a recording from its cover, she set it on her record player and pushed a button. A man's voice filled the room, singing *"Gloria in Excelsis Deo. . . ."*

Then she wound strings of lights around and around the tree. Lifting an imaginary glass in toast to the voice that hung in the air, she said, "Your voice is as lovely as ever. You are always here to visit every Christmas Eve. Thank you, my dear Thomas."

From the box, she lifted a doll with silver wings made by tiny hands from the box, saying softly, "Oh, Angie, my little angel, I wonder where you are tonight. I wonder about all the places you have been since you gave me the doll you made on the day your mother had to move because the rent came due."

Ms. Mac placed the doll on the highest branch of the tree and stood admiring its wings. "I only pray that you found a way to share your voice of an angel, the voice we heard only on the lunchroom stage that glorious Christmas concert when you sang 'Bring the torch, Jeanette Isabella. Bring the torch to the stable. Run.' Tonight I hope you are giving to others that glorious gift."

Ms. Mac hummed to herself as she unwrapped a small box and lifted a tiny egg covered in exquisite jewels hanging from a silken thread.

Laughing out loud, she stood on tiptoe to place it right below the angel, and she shook her head, remembering.

"Oh, Patty and Bobby and Troy and Margaret, and dear little Boo, how can I ever forget you?

"'This is too expensive,' I told you that day. 'I can't accept such a gift from my students!'"

But Patty had protested, "It's from all of us, Ms. Mac."

"Our daddy's the garbage man," offered Boo, standing tall and proud. "He found a whole box of these someone had thrown away, so we thought we would give you one for Christmas, because we love you."

Ms. Mac remembered how difficult it had been not to smile as she said, "Then, of course, I must accept this lovely gift from all of you."

Then as she unwrapped a tiny wooden cake complete with candles, Ms. Mac took a lace handkerchief from her pocket and wiped a tear from her eye. She unfolded a scrap of newsprint with a ribbon attached to each side.

"Thank you," she whispered. "Thank you to all of you who gave me such a special Mother's Day that year. You made me feel that you were really all my children when you bought an ad in the local paper to wish me a happy Mother's Day and a happy birthday because that year they fell on the same day.

"And, Jan, who organized the birthday party, I remember that your mother died that spring. Thank you for giving me a tiny cake I can take out each year. Wherever you are, I thank you, and I send you love," she said, touching each tiny candle as she hung the cake on the tree.

"Oh, Charley Bob, how I remember you," she said, lifting a ceramic candy cane, brightly colored but crooked and misshapen. "You never felt safe anywhere. Put you in the middle of any group and the group was suddenly in chaos. But one day, you sat still long enough to make this for me in your art class. I only wish you had sat so still that night when the police caught you climbing out the window of the bank. You might still be alive to know how I treasure your gift.

"I hope you feel safe at last," said Ms. Mac sadly. "I send you love on this night, wherever you are."

Pushing aside the tissue paper, Ms. Mac found a red ribbon with an airline captain's wings attached.

"And, Herbie, the president of my choir, you brought me your captain's wings when you took me to dinner the day you made captain," said Ms. Mac, smiling. "It was one of the proudest days of my life. Wherever you are, somewhere flying over this big wide world, I thank you, too. These wings remind me of you every year."

One by one, Ms. Mac lifted the gifts, each reminding her of a special student in her life, and placed them on the tree. She visited with each of them until the room was filled with memories.

"Everyone thinks I am lonely on Christmas Eve," she told her friends gathered around the tree. "How could I be lonely with so many friends like you to visit me? Thank you, my lovely children, for leaving a part of yourselves for me to cherish."

Finally, Ms. Mac turned on the Christmas lights, making the ornaments seem to dance. And then she sat in her cozy chair with the flowered cover, listening to the voices of her students, all in their childlike forms from long ago, surrounding her in the twilight. She smiled as she watched them enter the room. Angie. Patty. Bobby. Troy. Margaret and dear little Boo. Jan. Charlie Bob. And Herbie and Thomas. They crowded around her chair.

"Oh, yes, I have plans every Christmas Eve," she whispered. "Each year on this night, I have guests who have shared their lives with me. I have loved being your teacher," she said. "I have loved being a part of your lives. I wouldn't have missed it for the world."

Deck the Halls

Traditional Welsh Carol

With vigor

Deck the halls with boughs of hol-ly, Fa-la-la-la-la, la - la-la-la.

'Tis the sea-son to be jol-ly, Fa-la-la-la-la, la - la-la-la.

Don we now our gay ap-par-el, Fa-la-la, la-la-la, la-la-la.

Troll the an-cient Yule-tide car-ol, Fa-la-la-la-la, la - la-la-la.

2. See the blazing Yule before us,
Fa-la-la-la-la, la-la-la-la.
Strike the harp and join the chorus,
Fa-la-la-la-la, la-la-la-la.
Follow me in merry measure,
Fa-la-la, la-la-la, la-la-la.
While I tell of Yuletide treasure,
Fa-la-la-la-la, la-la-la-la.

3. Fast away the old year passes,
Fa-la-la-la-la, la-la-la-la.
Hail the new, ye lads and lasses,
Fa-la-la-la-la, la-la-la-la.
Sing we joyous all together,
Fa-la-la, la-la-la, la-la-la.
Heedless of the wind and weather,
Fa-la-la-la-la, la-la-la-la.

Christmas in a Shoe box

Ella Joyce Stewart

In the 1950s and '60s, when my family were farmers living in eastern North Carolina, we celebrated holidays differently from people living in the towns and cities. Easter was the beginning of the farm season. Everyone knew Good Friday was garden-planting time. The Fourth of July marked the beginning of putting in tobacco. That was when tobacco was brought out of the fields and cooked in barns. Thanksgiving meant no more hard work in the fields. And at Christmastime we didn't hang out stockings by the chimney with care. We brought out the shoe boxes.

During the year when one of us got a pair of shoes, Mama said, "Don't throw that shoe box away; Christmas is coming!" So it was put under my parents' bed with the other shoe boxes. A few days before Christmas, Mama said, "Somebody go in our bedroom, look under the bed, and bring out the shoe boxes." While my brothers went into the woods to cut down a Christmas tree, Mama sat with Daddy's red marking pencil. She wrote each child's name on a shoe box, starting with the youngest. There was Jacqueline, Victor, Kay, Faye, Glenda, Hillery, Brenda, Joyce, and Jimmy. In 1961, although they were living away from home, there were shoe boxes for my brother Tyson Jr. (T.J.) and my oldest sister, Minnie Larine. And of course there was a shoe box for Lillie and Tyson, which simply read "Mama & Daddy." They were all placed around the tree.

Early on Christmas Eve morning, Daddy and Mama went to town. We children got busy. We put an extra, extra cleaning on those walls and floors of the little plank house we called home. The shoe boxes were dusted inside and outside. We wanted to make sure everything was squeaky clean for old Saint Nick.

Christmas found us up at four o'clock in the morning. Who could sleep? Tinsel was hanging from the pine tree, along with the homemade construction paper rings. The shoe boxes were overflowing. In each were apples, oranges, nuts, loose raisins, hard candies, chocolate drops, a Bible coloring book, a puzzle book, socks, underwear, puzzles, and a handball paddle or a yo-yo. Daddy made a little extra money that year so the girls got a tea set and the boys got a bicycle. They didn't even mind sharing. Mama told us years later that the tea set cost $1.99, and the bicycle was a third-person hand-me-down repainted by Daddy. Did we care? It was a great Christmas for the Stewart children. It was like eating the smothered chicken after sopping up the gravy with the biscuits.

All day long we ate out of our shoe boxes, put together our puzzles, colored our Bible coloring books, drank tea, and rode the bicycle. In all the years of growing up on the farm, I don't remember wanting anything we didn't get. What we wanted most was the magic of Christmas and our shoe boxes of goodies.

At the end of the day, my sister Brenda said, "We have waited all year for Christmas; now Christmas done come and gone."

And Mama said, "That's right, Brenda, Christmas may be over, but Jesus lives on."

"Amen!" said Daddy. "Let the house say Amen!"

Miracle at Midnight

Katherine Paterson

When she was just a tiny little girl, her grandmother had told her a wonderful story. "On Christmas Eve at the stroke of midnight," she had said, "all the animals kneel down to worship the Baby who was born in a stable." Last year and the year before, Sarah had tried to stay awake to see the miracle, but this year, even though she dropped off to sleep as usual, she woke with a start. The numbers on her clock glowed in the dark room—11:35. She hadn't missed it.

She put on her long underwear, corduroy pants, and a heavy sweater. On top, she pulled on her ski pants. Then she tiptoed down the stairs. In the kitchen she added her snow boots and ski jacket.

There was fresh snow outside, but she stomped a path through it to the barn. A flashlight! She'd forgotten a flashlight. She started to go back to the house when she realized there was a light on in the barn. Old Joe, the hired man, must be up. Her heart sank. Joe would send her home to bed if he caught her. She mustn't let him see her. That was all.

She stretched up on her toes and pulled open the high heavy wood door. It creaked.

"Who's there, eh?" Old Joe's voice called.

Sarah just stood inside, breathing hard, waiting for him to call out again, but he was mumbling under his breath about something and didn't speak out. She didn't dare close the door. It was too noisy. Slipping toward her left, she started to climb the rolled bales of hay stored close by.

"Jeezum crow!" She was so startled she nearly fell. "Shut the dad-blamed door!"

Old Joe knew she was here. No use trying to hide.

She climbed down, waiting for him to send her back to the house. "I said, shut the dad-blamed door." She pushed the door to. "Who is it anyway?" Sarah walked out of the shadows.

Joe was standing in a lambing box. He was taller than the bright lights shining into the enclosure. He squinted down at her. "You, missy? What are you doing up this time a' night?"

She didn't answer. When Old Joe yelled, she felt too shy to speak. Anyhow, it was silly, wasn't it? Miracles didn't really happen in Vermont in the twenty-first century. That was only some old story of Grandma's.

"Well, cat got your tongue, missy? Speak up. Whatcha doing here?"

She stammered. "I wanted to see if the animals bowed down at midnight."

"Never heard such a thing. Now, get on to bed."

No use to argue. Sarah nodded and started for the door.

Just then the ewe in the lambing box gave out a loud bleat. Joe dropped to his knees. "Merciful heavens, Ethel. Don't tell me you're going to deliver hind legs afore. We're both too old for this kind of nonsense."

The ewe continued to bleat. The other animals in the farm began making stomping, restless noises. From the far corner, Sarah's pony neighed as if in sympathy.

Joe's voice turned quiet and soothing, almost like her mother's did when she was trying to calm the baby. "There, there, Ethel," he said. "I didn't mean to yell. I know you're doing your best. Now, now, take her easy. Old Joe ain't gonna let anything happen to you."

He had forgotten all about her. Sarah turned from the door and tiptoed back. As many animals as had been birthed on the farm since she herself had been born, she'd never actually seen it happen. She stood in the dark behind the lights and watched. Old Joe had turned into someone she's never known, tenderly coaxing the distressed ewe as he pulled gently on the awkward skinny back legs of the lamb Ethel was straining to deliver.

Sarah lost all track of time. She wasn't even sure she continued to breathe. She'd heard Joe and her dad talk about lambing and how hard it was when the lamb decided to come back legs first. But, finally, finally, Joe had a tiny wet lamb in his big hands.

Ethel turned her head, nudging Joe's hands as he carefully wiped the lamb's nose and mouth clean, put his own head down on the lamb's back to listen to its breathing. At last he turned the lamb over to Ethel, who began to lick her baby as though all the work of giving birth had been nothing at all.

Joe sat back on his heels. "There you go, Ethel, I knowed you could. I knowed you could." For a long time he watched the old ewe cleaning her lamb and then he threw back his gray head and laughed.

Sarah couldn't help herself. "Joe, you're laughing!"

"Huh?" Joe narrowed his eyes against the light. "You still here? I thought I told you a hour ago to go back to bed."

"An hour ago? Then it's past midnight!"

"Eyup. Well past. Santy Claus done come and gone."

"No. No. That means I missed the miracle."

"Now just what miracle was that, missy?"

"The one Grandma told me—about the animals all kneeling down. I wanted to see if it really happened. But I was so busy watching you and Ethel I forgot."

"Well, I guess I seen thousands of 'em, but every birth is a miracle to me," the old man said. Sarah looked down at the baby lamb, now up on its wobbly legs, pushing at Ethel's side to find its first breakfast and then latching on and sucking contentedly.

It *was* a miracle, and she had seen it.

"Now you get on back to bed, missy."

"I will, Joe. Merry Christmas."

But Joe was too busy tending to his sheep to answer.